W9-BYI-150

How to Lose
All Your Friends

by Nancy Carlson

Viking

VIKING
Published by the Penguin Group
Penguin Books USA Inc., 375 Hudson Street, New York, New York 10014, U.S.A.
Penguin Books Ltd, 27 Wrights Lane, London W8 5TZ, England
Penguin Books Australia Ltd, Ringwood, Victoria, Australia
Penguin Books Canada Ltd, 10 Alcorn Avenue, Toronto, Ontario, Canada M4V 3B2
Penguin Books (N.Z.) Ltd, 182–190 Wairau Road, Auckland 10, New Zealand

Penguin Books Ltd, Registered Offices: Harmondsworth, Middlesex, England

First published in 1994 by Viking, a division of Penguin Books USA Inc.

5 7 9 10 8 6

Library of Congress Cataloging-in-Publication Data

Carlson, Nancy L.
How to lose all your friends / by Nancy Carlson.   p.   cm.
Summary: Offers advice on the kinds of things to do if you don't
want to have any friends.
I S B N 0 - 6 7 0 - 8 4 9 0 6 - 5
[1. Behavior—Fiction. 2. Friendship—Fiction.] I. Title.
PZ7.C21665Ho 1994   [E]—dc20   92-28368 CIP AC

Printed in Singapore   Set in 20 pt. Madison

For Kelly, Pat and Mike,
because sometimes
their mother is a crab!

If you don't want to have any friends,
follow these simple instructions:

1. Never smile

Be gloomy.

Be cranky.

Frown a lot.

Being gloomy and cranky, and frowning
will scare off any friends!

2. Never share

If you are eating cookies, hide them
when your friends come over.

You could also stuff them all in your mouth,
or you could just run away.

When you're playing with toys, grab
all the good ones for yourself.

Then throw a tantrum if somebody else
plays with one of them.

You can also just lock everyone
out of your bedroom.

3. Be a bully

Pick on little kids.

Push in front of the lunch line.

Play mean tricks on kids.

4. Be a poor sport

When you play tag and someone tags you,
lie, and say they missed.

Cheat at cards; if you're losing
a board game, knock off all the pieces.

5. Tattle

Tell on kids when they run in the hall.

When your brother
makes a face at you,
tell your mom.
If your brother is
in Time Out, make
sure he stays there.

Now if you still have friends after all that,
I have one more lesson.

6. Whine!

Whine when it's too hot outside.
Whine when it's too cold outside.

Whine for treats.
That will irritate everyone.

If you follow these instructions you'll
be able to eat all the cookies you want.

And you will have no friends

to bother you.